Theseus
The Hero's Journey

Greek Mythology for Kids! Volume 1

By Eric Z

This is a work of fiction. Similarities to real people, places, or events are entirely coincidental.

THESEUS - THE HERO'S JOURNEY

First edition. February 10, 2024.

Written by Eric Z.

Which HERO are YOU?
Take the Quiz!
It's FUN and it's FREE!

THESEUS

HERCULES

PROMETHEUS

PERSEUS

SCAN HERE FOR THE QUIZ!

KidsBooks.Club

3

Table of Contents

THESEUS IN ANCIENT GREECE
Procrustes
Marathonian Bull
X
Cercyon
Crommyonian Sow
Sciron
Athens
Sinis
Periphetes
Troezen
NAXOS
X Ariadne
Fights the Minotaur!
Knossos
CRETE

Chapter 1: Theseus and the Secret of the stone

A long time ago King Aegeus of Athens went to the island of Troezen and visited his old friend King Pittheus.

King Pittheus had a beautiful daughter named Aethra, and Aegeus quickly fell in love with her.

King Pitheus and Aethra:

Aegeus and Aethra had a son named Theseus. Now King Aegeus would have stayed on the island of Troezen forever with his new family and best friend King Pittheus, but while Aegeus was on Troezen, tragedy struck Athens—the evil King Minos of Crete was attacking!

Aegeus had to go back to his kingdom in Athens to lead his army against King Minos. But he couldn't take his new wife and child with him. Aegeus was worried for their safety. Athens was at war, and he didn't want to expose his new family to such a danger.

So King Aegeus told his wife Aethra: "Under the huge stone in the forest, I have hidden my sword and a pair of new sandals. When Theseus is strong enough to lift the stone, send him to me in Athens."

And so, King Aegeus left his family in safety on the island of Troezen with King Pitheus, as he went back to Athens to lead the battle against King Minos to defend his city against the invaders.

This made Aethra very sad. She didn't even know if Aegeus would come back. But, in the meantime their brand new son Theseus grew and grew!

He became a strong and tall young man. In fact, he was the biggest youth of all of Troezen. And being a growing young man, he of course became curious about his father.

However, whenever he asked his mother Aethra about his father she would always answer "When the time is right my son, you will meet him."

Theseus wasn't happy with this answer one bit.

It nagged at him and bothered him all the time, like a pesky little bee buzzing in his ear no matter where he went. He just couldn't stop thinking about it. Finally, when he was sixteen years old, he went to his mother again; "Mother, please tell me at last who my father is!"

"Come with me," she said.

She led him to the stone whereunder his father had hidden his sword and sandals.

"My son, when you can lift this stone, you can go forth and meet your father."

Theseus bent down and dug his fingers as far under the edge of the stone as possible.

He heaved and heaved with all of his might, but he just could not lift the stone.

8

This made Theseus sad, but at the same time it made him mad. He went to King Pitheus, who was like a grandfather to him and asked his advice. "King Pitheus, I tried with all my strength to lift that heavy stone, but I just couldn't do it. I feel so frustrated and ashamed. What should I do?"

King Pitheus looked at the young man with compassion. "My dear boy, do not be discouraged. All you need is a plan. Now listen to me carefully." King Pitheus, being a man of great experience, leaned in and gave Theseus not only a plan, but an amazing idea…

The Secret Advice of King Pitheus:

After hearing this Theseus jumped up, now he was more determined than ever – he had a plan!

All the next year Theseus trained as hard as he could.

He imagined his goal in front of him at all times.

"By my next birthday, I will lift that stone!" he pledged to himself, and he made it known to all of his friends.

He trained every day from there on out.

He wrestled with his friends. He played all of the team sports at school and always volunteered to be the leader of the team, no matter what sport they played.

By the time of his seventeenth birthday, Theseus was ready to lift the stone.

He did not ask his mother this time, instead he said: "Mother, do not give me any birthday presents this year, the only thing I want is to lift that stone."

Theseus and his mother went to the stone again. This time Theseus looked at the stone angrily, and even said, "I'm going to lift you stone!"

He bent down and put his hands on each side of the stone.

He strained, he grunted, and the stone *seemed* to move a little bit!

But it didn't…

Theseus just couldn't lift it.

Panting, sweating, and dead tired, Theseus sat down dejected.

"Don't worry my son, I'm sure you will lift it next year," said his mother.

Theseus was embarrassed.

Now he had to go back to his friends—the same friends that he declared that he would lift the stone to.

This was the worst part.

Not only did he not get to meet his father, but he had to go back to school and admit failure to his friends.

But Theseus did not give up.

He went to his friends and told them what happened, and he added "But next year I will lift that stone—if it is the last thing I do!"

Theseus was now more motivated than ever in his life.

The humiliation of not being able to lift the stone, and the anger of still not knowing who his father is, spurned him on. As a matter of fact, everyone on the island said, "That is one driven young man!"

Theseus was obsessed with sports and leadership.

He began lifting heavy rocks and stone balls called "Atlas stones" after the famous Greek hero Atlas.

According to the legend, Atlas was so strong that he could bear the weight of the whole world on his shoulders.

Atlas was a symbol of great strength and endurance among the boys of Troezen.

Besides wrestling and team sports Theseus also started running—he not only wanted to be strong, but a hero also needs endurance.

Gradually Theseus got stronger and stronger. His hard work was paying off.

His friends said he had muscles like iron bands and a grip like stone.

He became famous in his school for being the strongest among them. Indeed, he had muscles like an adult!

Finally, Theseus's eighteenth birthday came.

He did not celebrate at all, instead he went straight to his mother and they both walked straight to "The Stone".

Theseus saw the stone in front of him.

The years of anger and humiliation boiled inside of him.

He envisioned himself lifting the stone and throwing it in the ocean.

He took a deep breath, he bent down once again, put his hands on the stone and gripped it, and with all his might, and focussed effort, he lifted the stone!

He wanted to pick it up over his head and throw it in the sea, but actually, it was still too heavy for that. Instead, he lifted it up and threw it to the side—revealing the marvelous sword and sandals!

His mother was moved to tears.

"My son! You did it! Now you can rightfully claim your birthright. The sword was put there by your father. He told me when you are finally strong enough to lift the stone, to send you to him."

But his mother still did not tell Theseus who his father was.

Instead, she said: "Now put on the sandals, and take this sword to Athens. Once you are there, go to king Aegeus. He will finally tell you who your father is. And remember: on your journey, always keep the sea on your right side, and watch out for bandits!"

Chapter 2: Trials and Adversaries

Theseus started on his journey from Troezen with the sword of his birthright in hand, his new sandals, and his heart filled with determination and the desire to prove himself.

And his mother was right about the bandits: As he made his way through the rugged terrain, he encountered the most hideous and dishonest thieves and bandits that would test his strength, skill, and courage...

One day, while walking along a dense forest, and always keeping the ocean on his right side, Theseus heard a thunderous noise echoing through the trees.

The path curved, and after the bend, in the middle of the path, he came face to face with a fearsome wildman.

It was Periphetes, known as "the Club Bearer," a fearsome bandit who terrorized travelers with his bronze club. His muscular frame and menacing grin sent shivers down the spines of those unfortunate enough to cross his path. Indeed, it was said that he killed everyone he came across and robbed them of their possessions.

PERIPHETES

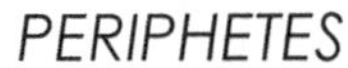

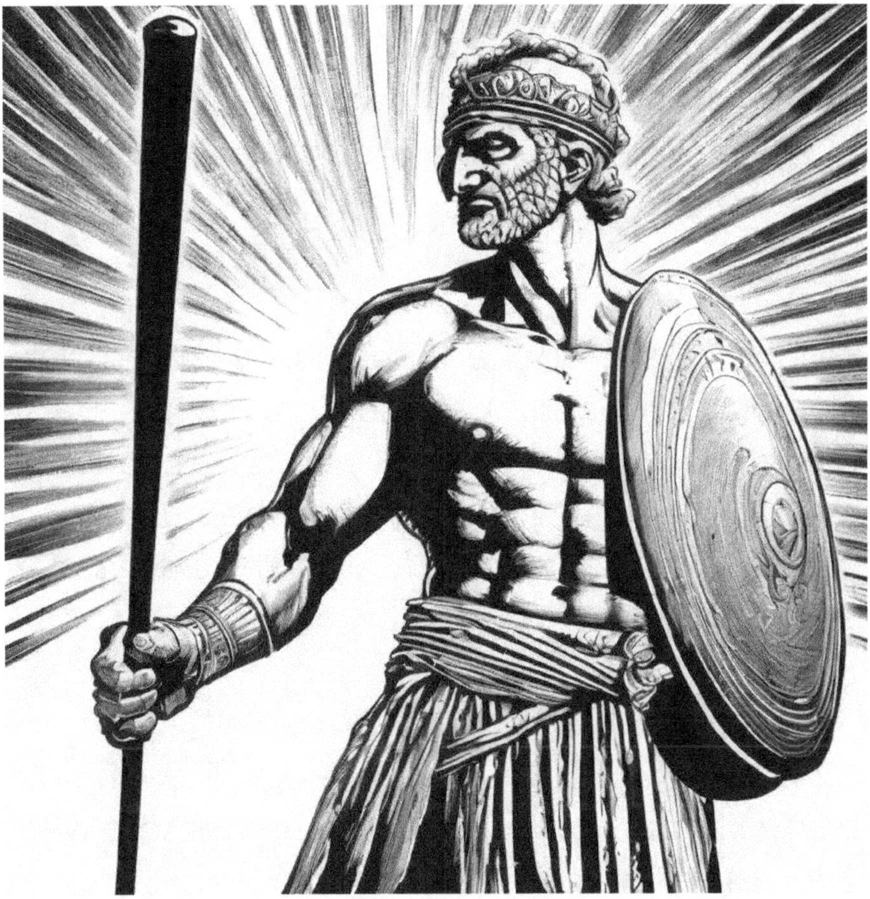

Unfazed by the bandit's reputation, Theseus squared his shoulders, his grip tightening around the hilt of his sword. He knew that defeating Periphetes would not only protect himself but also safeguard future travelers from Periphetes's evil ways.

unfazed

adjective

un-FAYZD

Not surprised or worried:

"She seems unfazed by her sudden success and fame."

Periphetes approached Theseus, his bronze club gleaming ominously in the sunlight. With a wicked grin, he taunted the young hero, attempting to scare him. However, Theseus remained resolute, his eyes fixed on his adversary—he was staring him down!

Periphetes stared back.

Suddenly, without warning, the bandit swung his club with raw power!Trying to crush Theseus with each strike, the battle was fierce.

But Theseus, agile and quick-witted, dodged the blows with grace using his superior speed and reflexes to his advantage.

The years of wrestling and practice sword fighting with his friends had trained Theseus just for this moment.

As the fight raged on, Theseus tried a move he had been practicing with his friends during their sword fighting classes:

As Periphetes got ready to throw his next blow, Theseus waited just a fraction of a second, and just as Periphetes swung his club, he stepped to the side and let Periphetes go by him, overextending his swing at the same time, which left Periphetes totally off balance. Periphetes realized his mistake too late as Theseus was now at his side ready to strike!

In a swift motion, Theseus grabbed Periphetes's club and struck him down with his own club!

"As you have done to others, so will I do unto you!" cried Theseus.

With Periphetes defeated once and for all, Theseus continued his journey, now with Periphetes's club as a trophy. Always keeping the ocean on his right side, he made his way toward Athens.

With each trial and adversary he encountered, Theseus grew stronger, both in body and spirit.

Little did he know that even greater tests awaited him on his epic journey.

Chapter 3: The Evil Sinis

Ancient Greece was no paradise. Throughout the land, vile and wicked scoundrels terrorized the innocent, preying on the weak and vulnerable. One such scoundrel was Sinis, also called "Pine Bender", a hulking brute of a man with the strength of ten oxen.

SINIS

Sinis had a most gruesome game: he would lure travelers to the forest, and then bend the trunks of towering pine trees to the ground. Once his unsuspecting victims were right between the bent trees, he would release them, letting the trees snap back upright and smash into the poor travelers. This would hurl the travelers into the sky, or even rip them apart!

Such a fate had befallen many an unwary traveler, and the people of the land lived in constant fear of Sinis and his pine-bending ways. But Theseus, with his keen wit and unwavering courage, knew that this foul **villain** must be stopped.

villain

noun

VIL-uhn

A bad person who harms other people or breaks the law:

"He's either a hero or a villain, depending on your point of view."

And so, Theseus set out for the forest, determined to confront Sinis and put an end to his
reign of terror. When he finally came upon the
pine-bending brute, Sinis eyed him with a menacing glare, no doubt expecting another hap-
less victim.

"So, you dare to challenge the mighty Sinis?" the
villain bellowed, his voice rumbling like thunder.
"Very well, then. Let us see how you fare against
the power of these mighty pines!"

With that, Sinis took the trunks of two towering
pine trees and began to bend them to the
ground, his muscles rippling the whole time. But
Theseus was not one to be afraid. Nope – he
had a plan!

As Sinis beckoned Theseus to come between the
bent trees, Theseus struck with the swiftness of a
viper. He grabbed the trees himself, his own
strength matching that of Sinis. And then, with a
mighty heave, he released his grip, allowing the
trees to snap back upright – this time with Sinis
caught between them.

The resounding crack of splintering wood and
the pitiful howl of Sinis the Pine Bender echoed
through the forest.

Sinis flew through the sky in a great arc. Who knows where he landed or if he survived? He was never seen again. It was the end of his reign of terror.

Theseus had emerged victorious, his cunning and witts triumphing over the brute force of his foe.

From that day on, the people of the land celebrated Theseus as a true hero, a champion who had delivered them from the clutches of the dreaded Sinis.

And so began the legend of the mighty Theseus, whose adventures had only just begun.

Chapter 4: The Crommyonian Sow

After his victory over the evil Sinis, Theseus continued on his journey, determined to vanquish any other monsters or threats to the people of Greece.

His next challenge would be the terrifying Crommyonian Sow.

The Crommyonian Sow was an enormous, savage wild boar that had been terrorizing the countryside around the town of Crommyon. This monstrous swine was massive, with razor-sharp tusks and an **impenetrable** hide.

impenetrable

adjective

im-PEN-uh-truh-buhl

Impossible to see through or go through: *"Outside, the fog was thick and impenetrable.."*

It would rampage through the fields, destroying crops and attacking any farmers or travelers that crossed its path.

The people of Crommyon had tried in vain to hunt down and kill the Crommyonian Sow, but the beast seemed unstoppable. They had even called upon the bravest warriors to try and slay the creature, but none had succeeded.

One time, a brave farmer who had had enough of the big pig's problems, decided to hunt it down and kill it.

He spotted it one day on his farm. Once the monster pig saw him it bolted for the wheat field. The farmer followed it into the wheat field with only his spear.

Once in the field the Crommyonian sow turned around and with a wicked whip of her head, she buried her sharp tusks in the back of the farmer's leg. She threw him with a strong thrust of her head and the farmer went flying out of the field! The injuries to the farmer were so bad that he later died.

Helpless, the townsfolk lived in constant fear, wondering when the Sow would strike again.

When Theseus heard about the Crommyonian menace, he knew he had to act. Grabbing his trusty sword, the young hero set out to track down the monstrous wild boar and put an end to its rampage.

It didn't take long for Theseus to catch sight of the Crommyonian Sow.

The beast was even larger and more fearsome up close, its beady eyes filled with wild aggression.

Theseus steadied his grip on his sword and charged straight at the Sow, letting out a mighty battle cry.

The Sow turned and charged at Theseus, its massive hooves pounding the ground.

But the young hero was too quick – he easily dodged the Sow's first attack, then he struck out with his sword with all his strength, sinking the point deep into the beast's side.

The Sow roared in pain, whirling around to face Theseus again.

It slashed at him with its deadly tusks, but Theseus continued to dart and weave, always staying one step ahead of the rampaging creature.

After a long and grueling battle, Theseus saw his chance. As the Sow prepared to charge him once more, the hero braced himself, then leapt high into the air.

With all his might, he plunged his sword straight down into the top of the Sow's head!

The Crommyonian Sow let out one final, agonizing squeal and collapsed to the ground...defeated at last.

Theseus stood victorious, panting heavily but filled with pride at his accomplishment.

From that day on, Theseus's triumph over the Crommyonian Sow was added to the legends and tales of his heroic deeds.

His bravery and skill had once again saved the people of Greece from a fearsome threat.

Chapter 5: The Encounter with Sciron

As Theseus continued his perilous journey, he found himself on a treacherous path that wound along the edge of a steep cliff overlooking the sea.

It was there that he encountered Sciron, a notorious bandit who delighted in tormenting unsuspecting travelers.

Sciron, a towering figure with a menacing smirk on his face, approached Theseus with a look of **arrogance** and superiority.

arrogance

noun

AIR-uh-guhns

being unpleasantly proud and behaving as if you are more important than other people:

"He has a self-confidence that is sometimes seen as arrogance."

Once Theseus walked up to him he had a strange request.

In fact, he demanded that Theseus wash his feet!

This was his cruel and evil custom: as victims knelt to wash his feet, he would kick them off the cliff to drown in the sea.

Now why would anyone wash his feet?

Well this Sciron was no ordinary bandit. He was known as "The Giant Sciron".

He was so big, nobody would even think of fighting with him in hand to hand combat.

He was heads above the rest, taller than any man in the land. So when he caught innocent travelers on the road, and demanded that they wash his feet, they thought they were going to get away easily, without being killed or robbed.

But this time it was Theseus.

Knowing that a direct confrontation with Sciron would probably result in being kicked off the cliff, Theseus chose to outwit the bandit and turn the tables instead.

Acting like many poor travelers before him, Theseus stooped down as if to wash Sciron's feet.
Then, quickly using all of his wrestling skills, he
grabbed Sciron by both legs and threw him to
the ground!

Sciron howled in pain and scrambled to regain
his footing, but in doing so, he lost his balance
right on the edge of the cliff.

Seizing the opportunity, Theseus swiftly stepped
aside, allowing the bandit to plunge into the un-
forgiving depths of the sea below. The tables
had turned, and it was now Sciron who fell off
the cliff.

The waves crashed against the rocks as Sciron met his watery death, bringing his cruel reign of terror to an end. The legend goes that Sciron smelled and tasted so bad that even the ocean spit him out. But Theseus did not stick around to watch that.

Theseus knew that he had not only saved himself, but also many others who would have fallen victim to Sciron's evil ways.

With Sciron defeated, Theseus continued his journey.

He understood that each challenge, no matter how **perilous,** was an opportunity for him to prove himself and gain experience along the way. And whenever he doubted himself, he would think of the advice from King Pitheus and press on.

---

perilous

adjective
PAIR-uh-luhss
extremely dangerous:
"The country roads are quite perilous."

Chapter 6: The Defeat of Cercyon

As Theseus ventured into the region of Eleusis, he learned of a formidable **tyrant** named Cercyon, who ruled Eleusis with an iron fist.

> ## tyrant
> *noun*
> TIGH-ruhnt
> **a cruel and oppressive ruler.**
> *"the tyrant was deposed by popular demonstrations"*

He challenged all newcomers to a wrestling match.

Cercyon's immense strength and famous wrestling skills struck fear into the hearts of all who encountered him.

But wrestling was also Theseus's favorite sport, and he looked forward to testing his skills on the most fearsome and famous wrestler in the land, Cercyon.

Determined to bring an end to Cercyon's tyranny, Theseus prepared himself for the wrestling match.

The news of Theseus's arrival spread quickly, reaching the ears of Cercyon himself. The tyrant, confident in his abilities, quickly challenged Theseus to a wrestling match.

He relished the chance to prove his dominance once again in front of all of his fellow Eleusians.

 The stage was set for an epic clash between two mighty warriors:

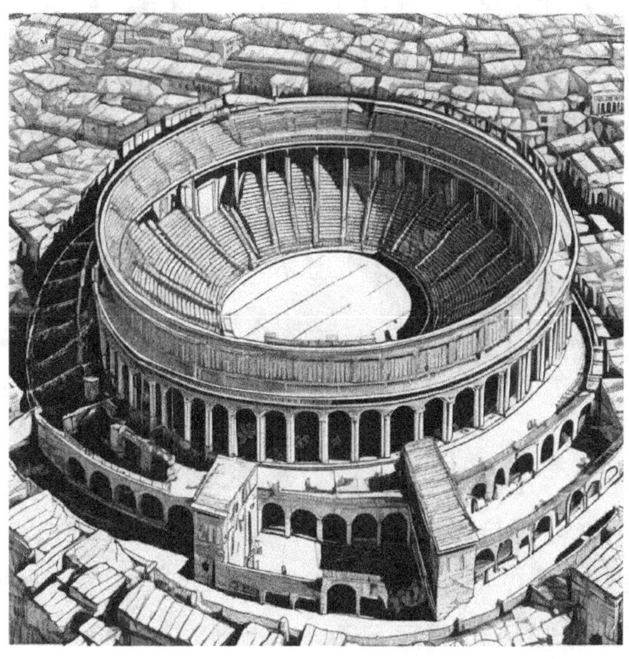

The wrestling match took place in a huge arena. There were hundreds of people watching them. They held their breath in anticipation as Theseus and Cercyon entered the middle of the arena floor, squared off and stood face to face, their eyes locked in a fierce gaze, each aware of the formidable opponent before them.

With a thunderous roar, the match began. Theseus and Cercyon circled each other…the crowd erupted in applause as the two warriors grappled, their muscles straining and their bodies locked in a fierce struggle.

Cercyon, relying on his raw power, attempted to overpower Theseus with his brute force. But Theseus, fueled by his determination and unwavering spirit, countered each of his moves.

As the wrestling match wore on, Theseus began to gain the upper hand, not only was his youthful energy an advantage, but his skill and intelligence proved to be the key to victory. With each hold and throw, he showed his mastery of wrestling, outmaneuvering Cercyon and exploiting his weaknesses.

The crowd watched in awe as Theseus demonstrated not only his strength but his wrestling skills too–he truly was an expert wrestler. And Cercyon had never been defeated before! They couldn't believe their eyes...

With a final, decisive throw, Theseus slammed Cercyon to the ground and pinned him with his iron grip. Cercyon was done...defeated at his own game!

The arena erupted in cheers and applause, the people of Eleusis rejoicing at the defeat of the arrogant Cercyon. Theseus emerged victorious, freeing Eleusis from Cercyon's tyranny and restoring hope to the people.

When Theseus left Eleusis, people were already talking about him as if he were a hero. But it takes a lot more than wrestling to make you a hero...

Chapter 7: The Bed of Procrustes

As Theseus continued his journey towards Athens, he came upon a notorious bandit called Procrustes, whose evil methods were infamous throughout the land:

Procrustes, also known as "the Stretcher," would invite weary travelers to rest in his house, only to trap them in his gruesome bed.

If the traveler was too tall for the bed, he would chop his legs off to make him fit.

And if the traveler was too small for the bed, he would stretch him to fit the bed!

This torture usually left the poor traveler hurt and misfigured, or even dead...

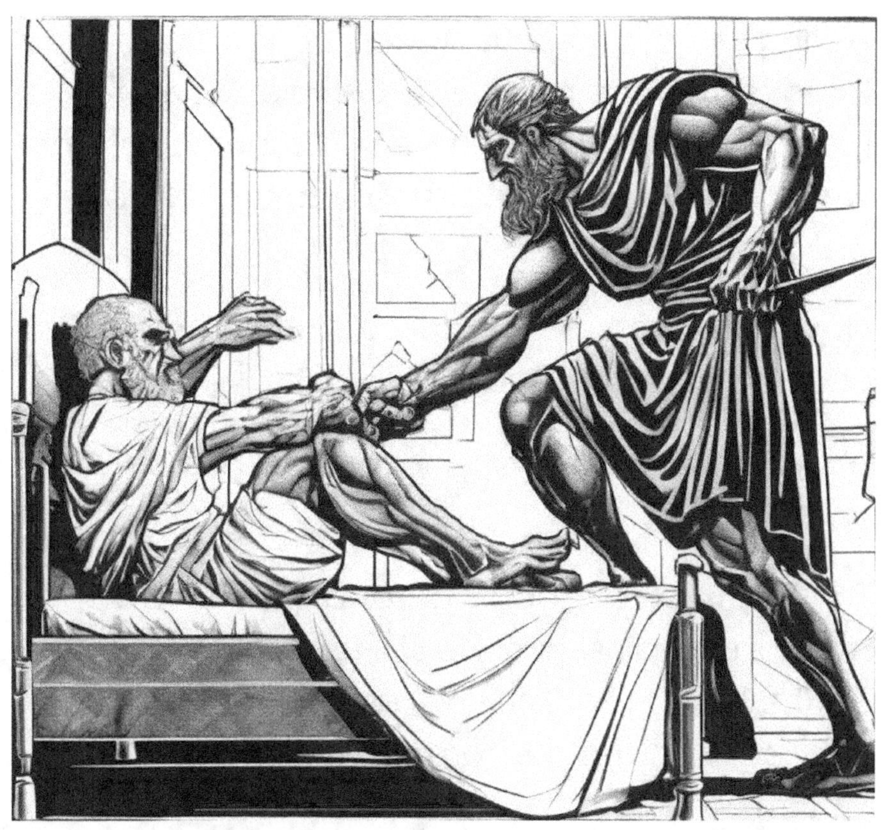

Word of Procrustes's atrocities reached Theseus, filling him with a determination to bring an end to the bandit's reign of terror.

With a strategic plan in mind, Theseus approached Procrustes's house, ready to outwit and defeat him.

Upon entering his house, Theseus found himself face to face with Procrustes, who, true to his nature, offered hospitality to the weary hero. Seizing the opportunity, Theseus cunningly turned the tables on Procrustes.

Acting sleepy, Theseus accepted Procrustes's offer to rest on the notorious iron bed. However, as Procrustes prepared the bed, Theseus leapt up with a sudden burst of strength and swiftly overpowered Procrustes.

Now in control, Theseus forced Procrustes to lie upon his own iron bed.

"As you have done to others, so will I do unto you!"

Theseus twisted Procrustes, and used his own methods against him. He stretched the bandit on the bed, Procrustes howled in pain! He experienced firsthand the torment he had done to his victims.

With Procrustes defeated and justice served, Theseus continued his journey towards Athens.

Unknown to him, his journey would take a more wicked turn.

Chapter 8: Athens at Last!

Wicked, because in the magnificent city of Athens, an evil witch was waiting for him!

After his long and tiring journey, the brave young Theseus finally arrived in the beautiful city of Athens.He let out a big breath, excited, yet tired at the same time. It was here that he must find King Aegeus and finally claim his rightful identity.

As Theseus made his way towards the grand and imposing palace, he encountered King Aegeus's wife, the powerful and treacherous witch known as Medea.

Medea was **infamous** for her cunning ways and dark magical powers.

infamous

adjective

IN-fuh-muhss

Famous for something considered bad:

"He's infamous for his bigoted sense of humour."

Medea knew that if Theseus were to meet with King Aegeus, the king might very well recognize him as his own long-lost son. And that would mean that Medea's son Medus could not become ruler of Athens, for Theseus would become the rightful ruler, taking his father's place. Medea simply could not let this happen. As she spoke, she quickly thought up a devious plan to kill Theseus.

Medea

"Oh no you don't! Who are you anyway?" she said.

"I am Theseus from Troezen. I have come a long way, and I have slain many evil bandits and monsters on the way to see King Aegeus."

"Really?" she said. "But I have not heard of you. Not anyone can see the king you know. If you are such a hero, as you claim to be, go get me the Marathonian Bull. Then I will gladly show you to the king."

Medea knew full well that the Marathonian Bull was a monstrous creature that had already killed everyone who crossed its path.

"Very well," said Theseus. "I will get your bull!"

Medea thought Theseus would never make it back alive, but she had woefully underestimated the young Theseus.

Chapter 9: The Marathonian Bull

With his trusty sword in hand, Theseus set off on his journey to Marathon. The evil Medea had challenged him to capture the bull, and he was determined to get it to finally see King Aegeus.

The sky darkened and a singular rain drop hit Theseus right on the nose. A pitter patter of rain drops suddenly became a full storm, blowing over trees and blasting sand in his face. Theseus ran to escape the storm, and went into the first house he could find. It was a small shack owned by an old lady named Hecale:

Theseus was a kind-hearted hero, and he treated the old lady with respect. He told her all about his mission: to capture the bull, and find out his true identity from King Aegeus.

Hecale was impressed by Theseus's bravery, and she had sympathy for the boy who did not know who he was. She made a promise to Theseus: she promised that if he was successful in capturing the Bull of Marathon, she would make a sacrifice to Zeus, the king of the gods.

ZEUS

Theseus thanked her for her support and went to hunt down the infamous bull.

Traveling north Theseus arrived in Marathon, where the bull was wreaking havoc, *again*. The Bull of Marathon was a huge, savage beast with massive horns and glowing red eyes.

It would charge through the fields, trampling the crops and scaring the villagers. The people had tried many times to capture or kill the bull, but it was far too strong and fierce for them to handle. The people of Marathon were terrified and needed someone to save them from this menacing bull.

But Theseus was not afraid. He had a plan!

First he went through the village and asked the farmers if he could have all the rope that they have. Then, armed with all of the ropes from the farmers, he approached the bull out in the field.

Using his quick reflexes and strategic thinking, he circled around the bull. The bull turned to Theseus and looked at him with those red burning eyes. He started churning the ground with his hoof, like bulls do when they get ready to attack. Suddenly he lowered his head and rushed at Theseus, snorting and thrusting his horns! One of the horns brushed right by Theseus's skin and caught his shirt and ripped a hole in it, but Theseus was able to pivot and let the bull go by, and at the same time he threw a rope around his neck!

The bull went into a rage and thrashed his head around, but Theseus pulled on the rope with all of his might. Now it is known among the farmers that when you pull a bull, it will pull back. And when you push a bull, it will push back in the opposite direction. Using this bit of farmers' wisdom, Theseus pulled as hard as he could on the rope. As sure as day follows night, the mean old bull started pulling against Theseus's pull. It was a tug of war between Theseus and the bull! The bull was so strong it backed up, pulling Theseus through the field like a plow.

Seizing this opportunity, Theseus yelled at the farmers, "Quick! Put the ropes around his legs!"

And, as the bull backed up, pulling Theseus the whole time, he stepped right into the ropes of the waiting farmers!

The bull bucked and went wild, but Theseus was so strong he held the bulls head down with his rope. Then he pulled the bull more towards the edge of the field and tied the rope to a thick post. Everytime the bull tried to buck or shake his head, Theseus would pull the rope even tighter. This shortened the rope each time, and gradually, the bull's head was right next to the post! He couldn't move his head at all. He was pinned so strongly to the post that he finally gave up, tired and exhausted. Theseus had captured the Bull of Marathon!

The people of Marathon rejoiced, for they were finally free from the bull's terror.

Theseus then led the captured bull back to Athens. The bull became known as the Marathonian Bull, named after the city where it was captured.

 Sadly, on his way back from Marathon, the old lady Hecale had died. Theseus was really grateful for her help. After her death he made sure that she received a proper burial. He also built a deme, which is a small community, in her honor because Theseus wanted to show his gratitude for her support and kindness.

Finally, Theseus gave the bull to the people of Athens who later sacrificed it. The bull's defeat became a symbol of Theseus's bravery and heroism, and the story of Theseus and the bull spread quickly throughout Greece.

Chapter 10: King Aegeus

After capturing the Marathonian Bull, Theseus returned to Athens. He went to the palace of King Aegeus, ready now to finally meet him.

As he approached the palace the guards crossed their spears and refused to let him enter. Medea, who was having tea and relaxing at the time, turned and saw him standing there. Her eyes widened and her jaw dropped like a rock. Her lips and eyebrows went into weird spasms and did a dance all over her face.

> ## spasm
>
> *noun*
>
> SPAZ-uhm
>
> **a sudden involuntary muscular contraction or convulsive movement.:**
> *"shifting heavy loads without help brought on muscular back spasms."*

She realized that Theseus had survived the Bull of Marathon!

Her face turned red with anger and hate. She turned to King Aegeus and said in a quavering voice, "There is that *strange* boy again, the one who demands to see you. I fear he is up to no good. Don't let him in!"

But, for the first time in a long time, King Aegeus ignored his wife's demand. "Is that the boy who claims to be a hero? The one who just captured the Marathonian Bull? Let him in!" responded King Aegeus.

The guards let down their spears and let him pass.

Queen Medea's eyes followed him every step of the way and widened with horror as Theseus sat down at the table, not too far from where King Aegeus was seated.

Though the king did not recognize Theseus as his own son, for there had been so many years since his birth and return to Athens, the wicked Queen Medea knew exactly who he was. And now she was desperate. Her emotions were cooking inside of her, but she tried to hide them. Her heart was pounding so hard that her necklace was

51

bouncing on her chest. The bull did not kill him, so she had to think of something else – really quick!

Secretly, under the table, Medea poured a deadly poison into a cup of wine.

She then handed the poisoned cup to Theseus and stood up tall.

With her sweetest, honey-dripping voice she proclaimed, "I propose a toast to our newcomer, and slayer of the Marathonian Bull, Theseus!"

She raised her own cup high.

Theseus, unaware of the evil ways of Medea, also rose to his feet and lifted the poisoned cup, ready to take a drink.

But just as Theseus was about to drink the deadly poison, King Aegeus noticed the sword that was hanging from Theseus's belt:

It was the very same sword that Aegeus had given to Theseus's mother, Aethra, many years ago, instructing her to hide it under a heavy stone, and only to give it to Theseus once he was strong enough to lift the stone.

Then he looked at Theseus's feet: he was wearing the sandals that he put under the stone too!

Upon seeing the familiar sword and sandals, a jolt of electricity rippled through his body, making his eyebrows shoot up and his lips part in a silent gasp. Time froze as he grappled with the shocking truth before him:

Theseus must be his long-lost son!

The joy, relief, and deep regret for all of the lost time with his son welled up inside of him and then he exploded: "My son!" he yelled. He swiftly knocked the poisoned wine right out of Theseus's hand and hugged him tightly, tears of pure happiness streaming down his face.

Theseus couldn't believe his eyes and ears when King Aegeus embraced him and declared him as his long-lost son. "I am the son of King Aegeus?!" exclaimed Theseus. He thought King Aegeus would tell him who his father is, he had no idea that King Aegeus *is* his father. After years of wondering about his true identity, he finally had the answer. He is the son of the king, and will be king himself one day!

The throne room erupted in cheers and applause as the kingdom celebrated Theseus's homecoming.

Theseus stood tall, his heart swelling with pride, as his father placed a crown upon his head, officially welcoming him as the prince of Athens.

"My son, I am overjoyed to have you back home where you belong," Aegeus said, his eyes shining. "Together, we will lead our people and bring peace and prosperity to our great city."

Theseus nodded, feeling a sense of purpose and belonging that he had never experienced before. He could hardly keep his emotions inside of him. He was truly bursting with joy. All the challenges he had faced, from battling the evil Sinis, to Cercyon and other bandits, and to capturing the Marathonian bull, all had led him to this moment.

Medea, however, saw the entire scene with empty eyes. Her heart sank in her chest and her disappointment was written in her face. She slowly and silently slipped into the shadows so no one would see her. She knew her plot to take over the kingdom with her son Medus was over.

As Theseus took his place beside his father on the throne, he knew that his journey was just beginning.

The fate of Athens rested on his shoulders. But despite this heavy burden, Theseus just thought of the advice from his mentor King Pitheus, and smiled…

He was ready to embrace his newfound role and use his bravery and intelligence to make a difference in the lives of the Athenian people.

Theseus ascended to the throne of his rightful father, taking his place as the true ruler of the magnificent city of Athens.

The End

But little did Theseus know, the challenges and trials of leadership are never truly finished. His real adventures were only just beginning…

↪

Your adventure continues here!

Join Theseus as he sails to the exotic island of Crete and battles the evil MINOTAUR **for life… or death!**

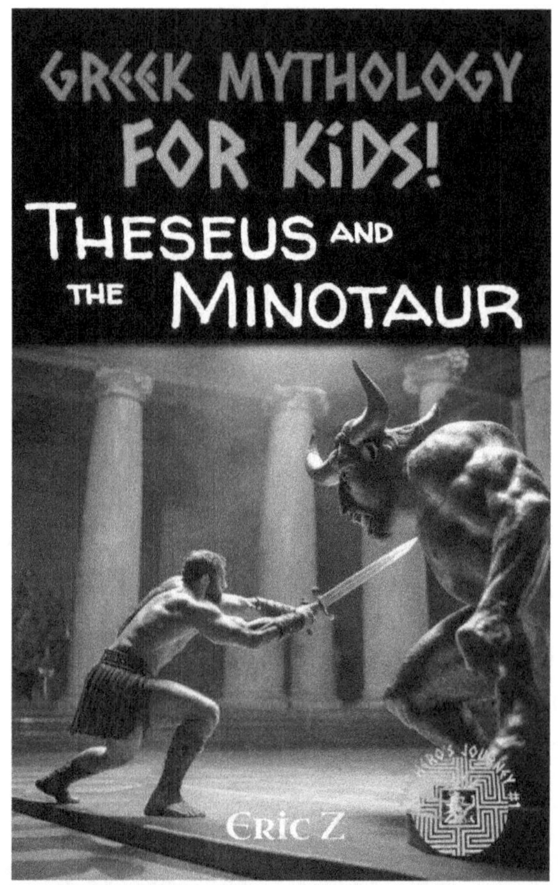

Join Theseus SCAN here!

Skip ahead!

Go straight to Book #3 – Hercules!

Get Hercules SCAN Here!

KidsBooks.Club

Study Questions

Character and Motivation:

1. Describe Theseus's personality. What are his strengths and weaknesses? Provide examples from the story to support your answer.
2. Why was Theseus determined to lift the stone? What does this tell us about him?
3. In the first chapter King Pitheus gave Theseus not only a plan, but an amazing idea. However the idea is never revealed in the story. What do you think that idea was?
4. How did Theseus's challenges and encounters with adversaries shape him into a hero?
5. Why did Medea try to poison Theseus? What does this reveal about her character?

Plot and Conflict:

1. What were some of the challenges Theseus faced on his journey to Athens? List at least three and explain how he overcame each one.
2. What was the significance of the sword Theseus found under the stone? How did it save his life?
3. Why do you think the author chose to include so many encounters with bandits

and monsters in Theseus's story? What purpose do these challenges serve?

4. How did Theseus's reunion with King Aegeus
   come about? What role did fate play in
   their meeting?

Themes and Symbols:

1. What is the significance of strength in "Theseus"? How is strength portrayed, and how
   does it contribute to Theseus's journey?
2. What lessons can be learned from Theseus's
   perseverance in overcoming obstacles?
3. How does the story explore the theme of
   identity? Think about Theseus's quest to find
   his father and his place in the world.
4. The sword Theseus received from his father
   can be seen as a symbol. What might the
   sword represent in the story?

Personal Reflection:

1. Which of Theseus's challenges did you find
   the most exciting? Why?
2. What qualities make Theseus a hero in your
   opinion?
3. If you could ask Theseus one question, what
   would it be?

BONUSES

What's Up with Those Outfits? Didn't Ancient Greeks Wear Pants?

Have you ever looked at pictures of the famous Greek hero Theseus and wondered, "What on earth is he wearing?"

It's true, the clothes worn by people in ancient Greece look nothing like the jeans, t-shirts, and sneakers that kids wear today.

Instead of pants, the ancient Greeks wore something called a chiton. A chiton was a long, loose piece of fabric, usually made from wool or linen, that would be wrapped around the body and pinned or belted at the waist. Over the chiton, men might also wear a cloak or shawl called a himation, which could be draped in different ways.

On their feet, ancient Greeks typically wore simple leather sandals or went completely barefoot. The whole outfit might seem strange to us, but the ancient Greeks found their draped clothing to be very practical and comfortable.

The free-flowing style of the chiton and himation allowed for easy movement, which was important for the active lives led by heroes like Theseus. The loose fabric also provided good cooling in the warm Mediterranean climate. And the chiton could be adjusted and rearranged as needed, making it a handy garment indeed.

So while the fashion of ancient Greece looks quite different from what we wear today, it served an important purpose for the people living back then.

Next time you see a picture of Theseus or another famous Greek hero, take a closer look at their distinctive outfits. You might be surprised by how skillfully they could wear those draped robes and cloaks!

LINK LIST:

1. https://www.kidsbooks.club/2024/05/which-greek-hero-are-you-take-this-quiz.html
2. https://www.kidsbooks.club/2024/05/your-adventure-continues-here-theseus.html
3. https://www.kidsbooks.club/2024/05/get-hercules-here-book-3-in-greek.html
4. Chapter 1: **THE AMAZING IDEA** https://bit.ly/SecretAdvice